06/07

PLANES

Catherine Ellis

PowerKiDS press™

New York

For Margaret, an invaluable consultant and good friend

Published in 2007 by The Rosen Publishing Group, Inc.
29 East 21st Street, New York, NY 10010

First Edition

Editor: Amelie von Zumbusch
Book Design: Greg Tucker

Photo Credits: Cover, p. 11 Shutterstock.com; p. 5 by U.S. Air Force; p. 7 by Master Sgt. Shaun Withers, Air National Guard; p. 9 by Senior Airman Brian Ferguson, U.S. Air Force; p. 13 © Aaron D. Allmon II/U.S. Air Force via Getty Images; p. 15 by SSGT Cherie A. Thurlby, U.S. Air Force; p. 17 © Chris Helgren-Pool/Getty Images; p. 19 by Tech Sgt. John K. McDowell, U.S. Air Force; p. 21 © U.S. Air Force/Getty Images; p. 23 by Chad Bellay, U.S. Air Force.

Library of Congress Cataloging-in-Publication Data

Ellis, Catherine.
  Planes / Catherine Ellis. — 1st ed.
      p. cm. — (Mega military machines)
  Includes index.
  ISBN-13: 978-1-4042-3667-7 (library binding)
  ISBN-10: 1-4042-3667-8 (library binding)
  1. Airplanes, Military—Juvenile literature. I. Title.
  UG1240.E448 2007
  623.74'6—dc22
                                        2006030159

Manufactured in the United States of America

Contents

Military planes are used to fight wars. These planes make up a country's **air force**.

Planes have wings. Air pushes against the bottom of a plane's wings. This keeps the plane in the air.

The front of a plane is called the nose. The back of a plane is called the tail.

Most military planes carry **weapons**. This plane has several weapons under its wing.

11

The person who flies a plane
is called the **pilot**.

This plane is a B-2 Spirit Bomber. Its shape lets it move through the air very quickly.

The Harrier can take off and land very quickly.

The E-3 has a **rotodome**. The rotodome gathers facts about other planes in the sky.

The F-117 Nighthawk often flies at night. Nighthawks are very hard to see and hear.

21

The Global Hawk does not carry a pilot! People on the ground direct this plane.

Words to Know

air force (ER FORS) The planes a country has to fight wars.

pilot (PY-lut) A person who works an aircraft, spacecraft, or large boat.

rotodome (ROH-toh-dohm) A rounded plate on top of a plane.

weapons (WEH-punz) Objects used to hurt or kill.

Index

Web Sites

Due to the changing nature of Internet links, PowerKids Press has developed an online list of Web sites related to this book. This site is updated regularly. Please use this link to access the list:
www.powerkidslinks.com/mmm/planes/